Dedicated to Tom Tom, My Puffin and
Evan, My Muffin.

PEP! SQUAD: 5 Seps to a Healthy and Happy Pet

ISBN: 978-0-692-65543-6

PEP! The Pet Education Project is an education and outreach program that teaches the core responsibilities of pet ownership. We strive to foster humane habits in children and citizens of our community in order to reduce pet overpopulation, abuse, neglect, and euthanasia.

To bring PEP! to your community visit www.ilovepep.org
Follow us on www.facebook.com/ilovepep & instagram @peteducationproject

The Author/ Founder would like to thank all our supporters, donors, board, and volunteers who make PEP!, happen and grow each day!

100% of the proceeds will go to PEP!, (a 501(c)3 non-profit organization).

Illustrated by Tina Modugno
www.tinamodugno.com

PEP! SQUAD

THE 5 STEPS TO A HAPPY AND HEALTHY PET

Welcome to the pet store!
It sits on the corner of Main Street
and has a bright green front door.

It's called the PEP! Shop.
It's a place where kids can learn a lot.

Pep!® Pet Shop

This is where the PEP! Squad lives.
They have knowledge about pets to give!

Pep!® PET SHOP

It's a warm summer day,
and all the PEP! Squad was ready to play.
Up they rose from their beds,
and headed downstairs to be fed.

In the kitchen the PEP! Squad sat down to eat
where they enjoyed their food, fresh water, and a treat.

Today we have a big surprise.
Someone special is stopping by.
Dr. Hamilton will be our special guest.
He is our town's local vet.
Pep!

"Oh no," said the PEP! Squad.
Pinky and Rufus quickly ran out of the room,
kicked up their food and knocked down a broom.
The broom flew onto the table and hit Mr. Poisson,
all while he was buttering his morning croissant!

Pinky poofed her fur, Rufus tucked his tail,
and they sat there nervously awaiting the door bell.
Oh dear PEP! Squad please don't fear.
Healthy pets see the vet just once a year!

Ding! Dong!
In walks Dr. Hamilton with a bag in his hands.
He has come today to do an exam.
Dr. Hamilton doesn't mean to scare.
He is coming over to talk about pet care.

"Our check up will be nice and quick.
Your yearly shot is just a stick.
That was not so bad, you see.
We're all done with the exam, now you are free.
But I must say one more thing before I go,
raising a happy and healthy pet is important for kids to know!"

Ok PEP! Squad, let's go have some fun!
Our PEP! Talk has now begun!
Today we will teach kids how to care for their pets.
So we're gonna break it down into 5 simple steps.

STEP 1 FOOD:

Feed your pets twice a day,
but not too much.
They'll stay healthy that way.

Did you know animal bones are not good for your pet?
Try a chew toy. It's a safer bet!
Certain foods like chocolate and raisins are not safe for pets to eat.
Always research before giving them a treat.

STEP 2 WATER:

Make sure they have water when they go out to play.
Fill their bowls up at least twice a day.
In the winter, water will freeze.
Rufus says, "No popsicles, please!"

Water evaporates when it's hot in the summer.
Empty water bowls are always a bummer!
Remember to keep their water bowls clean or
they will turn all nasty and green.

STEP 3 SHELTER:

Our pets need a place to sleep,
somewhere to call home,
and somewhere to count sheep.

Give your pets a fluffy bed
or a dog house
to rest their head.

Please don't chain your dog outside.
There are better ways to keep them safe and nearby.
Collars and tags are an important thing.
They like to wear them. It's their bling.
Microchipping is always a safe bet.
It's a great way to find a lost pet.

STEP 4 CARE:

Lots to do: spay, neuter, groom, and vet visits too!
Your vet will care for your pet when they are hurt or sick.
They will also help prevent against fleas and ticks.

Your pets need a bath just like you.
Keep them clean with pet shampoo!

Be sure your pets are neutered and spayed,
so they won't have babies, and run away.

Pets can have many kittens and puppies! Up to 16 a year!
There are already too many homeless animals! Oh dear!

Let's talk about animal shelters for a bit.
There are lots of animals for you to pick.
When looking for a pet, before you shop,
be a hero, and opt to adopt!
Many animals will never find a home.
It makes us sad that they're all alone.

There are lots of animals to meet and see:
dogs, cats, rabbits, and even parakeets.
1 in 4 shelter pets are pure bred pups.
Shelter pets are not just mutts!
From labradors to pugs, and boxers to shih tzus,
your new best friend is waiting for you!

Heartworms are an important subject to discuss.
Heartworm prevention is a must.
Your pet can catch heartworms from pesky mosquitoes.
They drink blood from your pet through their little bitty needles.
A heartworm pill once a month is all your pet needs
to keep them healthy and heartworm free!

Train your pet so they are well behaved.
It's best to start at an early age.

STEP 5 LOVE:

Before we go,
Love is the last step you need to know!
Your pets love you and want to be your best friend!
Pets want to have a forever home 'til the end.
Your pet likes to be petted and rubbed,
even talked to and loved.

Show your pets you love them everyday
by taking them out for a walk or to play!

Now that you know what your pet needs each day,
We just have one more thing to say!
If you want to be a part of our crew,
take the PEP! Pledge, that's all you have to do!
Food, Water, Shelter, Care, and Love;
Don't choose one, but all of the above!

PEP! PLEDGE

I pledge on this day, to take care of my pet in every way.
I will give him food, water, shelter, care, and love.
And lots of cuddles, treats, and belly rubs.
I promise to spay & neuter my pet,
and give them their shots when I take them to the vet.
I will be sure my pet is happy everyday,
keep them healthy, and never give them away.
My pet is my best friend,
and I promise to love and care for him till the end.

NAME ______________________ **DATE** ______________________

GLOSSARY

Vet: An animal doctor.

I.D. Tags: A tag that pets wear on their collars with contact information for their owner.

Microchipping: Is a permanent way to identify a pet. It is a small implant the size of a grain of rice that goes in the back of their neck.

Spay and Neuter: A small surgery your vet does to stop your pets from having babies.

Animal Shelter: A place where lost or homeless pets go to find a home.

Heartworms: A disease that dogs and cats can catch from mosquitoes where worms can grow and live inside their heart.

Heartworm Pill: A pill that you need to give your pet once a month to prevent heartworms.

CPSIA information can be obtained
at www.ICGtesting.com
Printed in the USA
LVIC06n1349091117
555635LV00003B/8